Jennifer Staromir

Willy and Lilly's
Adventures with Weather

CRISSCROSS
APPLESAUCE

www.BuffaloHeritage.com

JENNIFER STANONIS, Meteorologist
Illustrated by BILL BLENK

"Brrrr, it's WINTER!" Willy shivers.

"Should we go outside and play?"

2

Lilly sighs as she replies,
"Let's check the weather today!"

3

"The temperature is 32 degrees,
that's low enough for snow.

Chilly air is moving in
and icicles will soon grow."

4

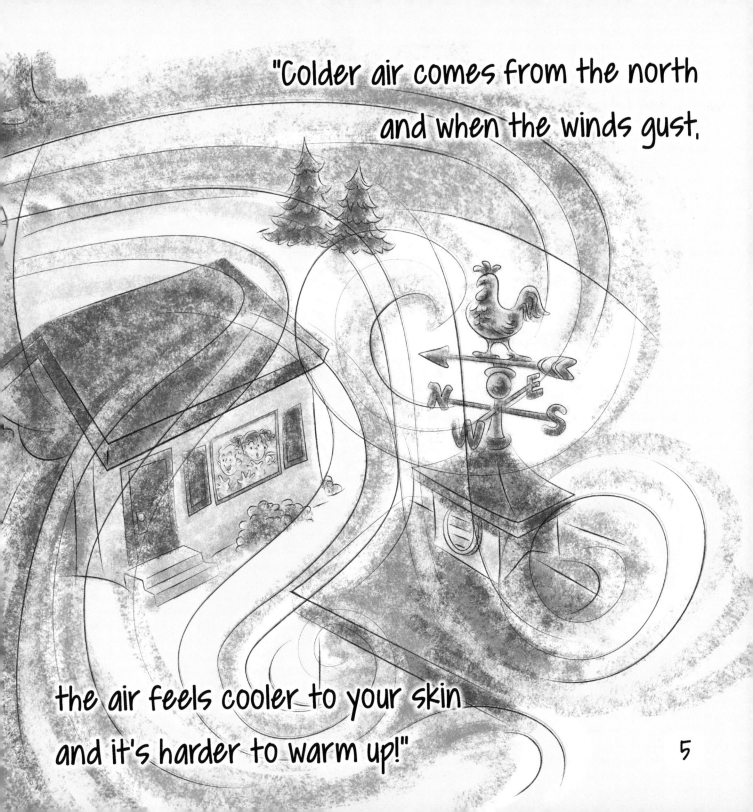

"Colder air comes from the north and when the winds gust,

the air feels cooler to your skin and it's harder to warm up!"

5

"Let's get our winter clothes-
jackets, boots, and gloves.

Soon we can sled, snowshoe and ski.
Outside, here we come!"

"OH!" says Lilly. "The sun is out
and some clouds are moving by.

See our long shadows on the ground
from the sun so low in the sky!"

7

"Watch out!" Willy points out.
8 "A cold front will come through!

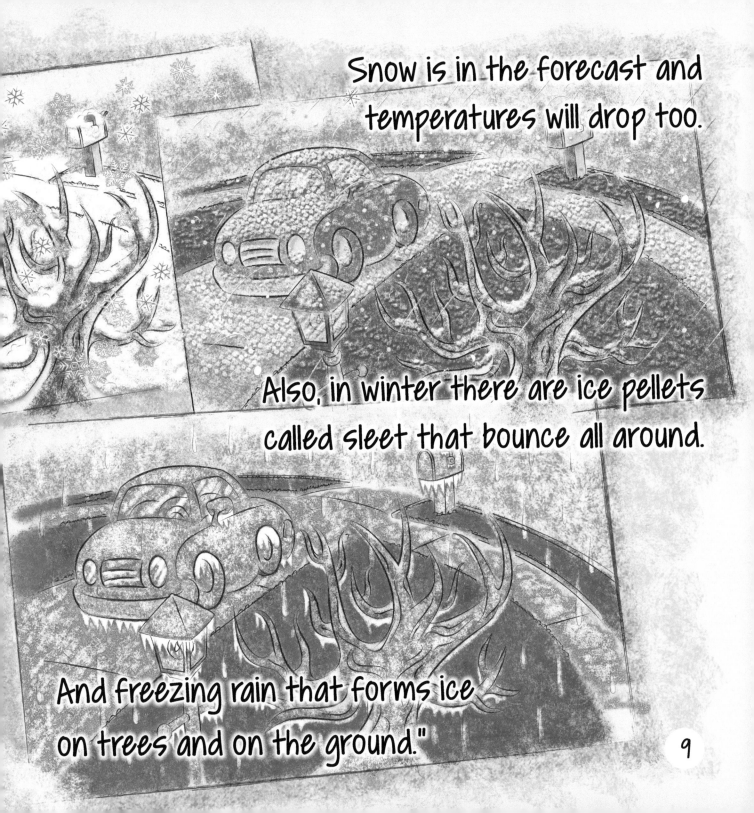

Snow is in the forecast and temperatures will drop too.

Also, in winter there are ice pellets called sleet that bounce all around.

And freezing rain that forms ice on trees and on the ground."

9

"Daylight will get longer

10 after the first day of winter.

The shortest day of the year
is on the Winter Solstice in December."

11

"Now it's SPRING!" Lilly sings.
"Let's go out and play!

12

The weather is getting nicer each and every day."

13

"Temperatures are warming up,
the snow has melted down.

Flowers now bloom everywhere
with colors all around!"

14

"We'll still have time to play,
since it won't be too dark.

Days keep getting longer
after the Spring Equinox in March."

"It's SUMMER!" Lilly shouts.
"I'm going out to play!"

"Wait!" says Willy. "It's hot out there.
We need to plan our day."

"The sun is warming up the land.
It's 95 degrees outside.

See our short shadows on the ground?
They're from the sun high in the sky.

"And OH!" Lilly warns.

"A warm front will move through!

We could see rain showers
And some thunderstorms too!"

27

Willy says, "But Lilly!
That's coming later tonight.

For now let's stay outside
and hope the forecast is right!"

29

"After the first day of summer daylight will get shorter soon.

The longest day of the year
is on the Summer Solstice in June."

31

"It's FALL!" announces Willy.
"We should head out to play!

Because the weather is already starting to change today."

"It's cooler and cloudy,
and look what I see," says Lilly.

34

"The leaves are changing color and falling quickly now.

And I see fog, low clouds near the ground."

36

"Tonight it will clear
and start to cool down.

Tomorrow we'll wake up early
to frost all around!"

"The days keep getting shorter after the Fall Equinox in September.

38

Our Earth keeps moving around the sun,
and soon again it will be Winter."

39

Willy and Lilly's
Weather Words

Cloud   A group of water droplets or very small ice crystals that float above the ground.

Dew   Tiny drops of water that form on surfaces when the air has high humidity.

Drizzle   Very small water drops that fall from a cloud.

Equinox   When the vertical rays of the sun are striking the equator and the lengths of daylight and darkness are the same. There are two equinoxes, one in September and one in March.

Fog   When a cloud forms at or very near the ground.

Forecast   A prediction of what the weather will be in the short or long term.

Freezing Rain   Rain that freezes when it lands on a frozen ground or surfaces, creating a layer of ice that is very slippery to walk or drive on.

Frost   Ice crystals that form on surfaces when the temperature is at or below freezing and winds are light.

Hail   Hard lumps of ice that form within and fall from thunderstorms, ranging from pea to softball size.

Heat Index	The temperature your skin feels when combining hot air with humidity.
Humidity	A measure of moisture in the air.
Lightning	A flash of light produced by the flow of electricity within a thunderstorm or between the thunderstorm and the ground.
Rain	Large water drops that fall from a cloud.
Sleet	Ice pellets that fall from a cloud (often mixed with rain and/or snow). Sleet forms when snowflakes begin to melt while falling through a layer of warm air and then refreeze into ice pellets while falling through freezing air near the ground.
Snow	Ice crystals (snowflakes) that fall from a cloud.
Solstice	When the vertical rays of the sun are either the furthest north or south of the equator. There are two solstices, one in December and one in June. The longest day of the year (length of daylight) is on the Summer Solstice and the shortest day of the year is on the Winter Solstice.
Temperature	Is a measure of hotness or coldness (the amount of energy in a substance). Temperature is measured in degrees often expressed in either Fahrenheit (F) or Celsius (C).
Thunder	The sound from a lightning strike as the air is rapidly heated.
Thunderstorm	A tall cloud that produces lightning and thunder, and often heavy rain, gusty winds, and small hail. Strong to severe thunderstorms could produce large hail, damaging winds and even tornadoes.
Weather	The state of the atmosphere at a given place and time, with respect to temperature, cloudiness, moisture, wind, air pressure, etc.
Weather Fronts	Boundaries that separates masses of warm and cold air.
Wind Chill	The temperature your skin feels when combining cold air with the wind.

MEET THE
Author

Meteorologist and Mom Jennifer Stanonis has covered and forecasted tornadoes, major snow storms, forest fires, floods, arctic blasts and more during her decades as a television meteorologist. The seeds that grew into *Willy and Lilly's Adventures with Weather* were sown while taking her twins on walks in all sorts of weather. A native of northern California, Stanonis has a degree in meteorology from SUNY at Brockport and a degree in broadcasting from San Francisco State University. She now resides in Buffalo, New York, with her husband and three young children.

MEET THE
Illustrator

When Bill Blenk isn't drawing he enjoys activities in all kinds of weather. He creates art and animation for local and national clients for print, broadcast and video game use, and also teaches visual and digital media arts and animation at area high schools and colleges. Whether riding his bike around Buffalo or heading down the slope on skis, he enjoys all four seasons in Western New York.

ISBN: 978-1-942483-47-2 (softcover)
ISBN: 978-1-942483-48-9 (hardcover)

www.BuffaloHeritage.com

Book design by Ana Cristina Ochoa
Printed in the United States of America

Published by CrissCross AppleSauce,
A Buffalo Heritage Press imprint
Buffalo Heritage Press
266 Elmwood Avenue, Suite 407
Buffalo, New York 14222
www.BuffaloHeritage.com

Library of Congress control number available upon request

10 9 8 7 6 5 4 3 2 1

CPSIA information can be obtained
at www.ICGtesting.com
Printed in the USA
BVHW021150241019
561935BV00001B/2/P